I0764364

A Knight's Quest for the Holy Grail

It's not always the quest for the cup.

Sometimes, it's the quest for what's in *the cup.*

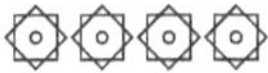

C. S. Johnson

STORY AUTHOR
C. S. Johnson
GRAPHICS ILLUSTRATOR
Fammy Purnama

This edition of the book includes a sample chapter of *The Heights of Perdition* (The Divine Space Pirates, Book 1) by C. S. Johnson.

I was too excited for the release of the book in 2018, but I would like to make the belated dedication.

This is only for you, Ryan my love. You are the pillow to my blanket, the fiddlesticks to my fudgenuts, and the cake to my icing. I did not know until I knew that my heart had been in search of you, but I am eternally grateful to God for helping us find each other.

AUTHOR'S NOTE

Dear Reader,

I've always been a bit surprised at how my life has turned out—or at least, how it's turned out so far. God has always been the god of irony to me, making me laugh at the world as much as I have to laugh at myself sometimes.

But there are quite a few sobering things about life and all the paradoxes that please and frustrate me along the way. Those of you who know me likely know the story behind this one, and I apologize for the reiteration; for those of you who don't, I hope you won't mind me sharing it here.

Several times throughout my life, I have dealt with depression. I have tried a few different paths with this, including stress management, medicine, and therapy. It's a hard path to walk, and I find that it's no surprising that the people who have enjoyed this story the most are people who struggle with some sort of mental illness. I've never been one to believe that you can walk away from your demons, any more than Jacob refused to let go as he wrestled with God. And while the pain is staggering to consider in hindsight, the joys I have found are just as amazing.

One such joy is the love of my husband. His patient lovingkindness and his steadfastness have offered a refuge I can only say is a matter of divine providence. To honor that, and to give my beloved a small token of my thanks, I wrote this story as a submission piece to an anthology. When it was rejected, I felt it was only right; in the end, it's something that can really only stand on its own. With the added illustrations courtesy of my artist friend Fammy, I am pleased to present this story to you in both its written and graphic forms.

Thank you, dear reader, as always, for allowing me to have a small slice of time in your life. I truly appreciate it, especially knowing this is a reflection of my heart, and my heart, as broken as it is, does not always offer such a pretty picture.

Until We Meet Again,

C. S. Johnson

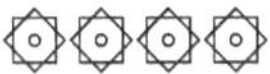

A Knight's Quest for the Holy Grail

Every knight has a quest, and every quest has its reward.

As a knight-errant, albeit one still in training, with only a year of service behind him, Lance took his duty seriously. But waking up was also a serious business, and that was why, despite the midmorning light flickering over his face, Lance was still half asleep. His faithful steed stepped up to help him, breathing smelly fumes into his face.

"Blah!" Lance sputtered, trying to clear his tongue of the frothy waft. "What have you been eating, Percy?"

His pet's pungent wake-up call forced Lance to roll over. When the heat of Percy's breath continued to eat into the shield of his pending sleep, Lance finally gave in to his beast's rude awakening.

"Alright, I'm getting up. Back from me, you fearsome brute."

The horse was far from intimidated by Lance's waking grogginess; instead, he moved closer to his master, nuzzling him with his wet nose.

"You're lucky you're the runt of your family," Lance grumbled, sitting up. He patted down his hair, brushing the chestnut locks out of his eyes, before taking in the full sight of the bouncing creature before him. "Or you would be tied outside, like the ones at my mother's house."

Percy gave a small yip, and the nuzzle became a nudge.

"Alright, alright," Lance muttered, petting his horse's long, flowing mane playfully. "I know you're hungry."

He also knew there was no point in trying to sleep when Percy was hungry—no matter how sleepy he still was.

"I suppose you're right, anyway, Percy." Lance yawned and rubbed his hands over his face. "We promised the princess we would save her today, and every knight knows there is nothing more important than completing his quest."

Lance tossed Percy several treats and stroked his pet affectionately, before he put on his armor for the day. He pulled a breastplate polished to a shine over his head, slipped his feet into protective boots, and even donned a helmet to protect his face from the bright summer sunshine.

Before too long, he stepped outside his quarters. Percy came trotting eagerly after him. With his steed at his side and a grin on his face, Lance set out into the morning to see his princess.

"Princess Alexandra, I am coming for you," he called out rapturously, eager to see his beloved once more.

Lance had met Alexandra at the university in the small kingdom of Torroa last year, on the very first day he arrived. Heading out to explore his intended home for the next four years or so, he had passed by several of the grand buildings, towering fortresses dedicated to learning, before he turned a corner, and his whole world turned on its head.

That was the moment he saw her.

Alexandra walked right by him, making her way toward the university library. Her small crowd of followers and friends were beside her, but she stood out from among the crowd immediately. There was a book in her hand, and she carried herself with a determined stride, her long hair flowing behind her as she headed into the hallowed halls of education, ready to change the world.

She had no way of knowing how much she had changed his world in that moment.

Transfixed by the contrast of her prim, petite figure and the multitude of the world's trouble before her, Lance followed Alexandra at a distance, before losing her in the labyrinth of Torroa's great library. Only when he gave up searching for her did he finally find her, sitting alone at a table covered with towers of books.

Lance could not name the exact moment he had fallen in love with her, but he knew the moment when he could no longer separate his happiness from hers.

It was several days and many discussions later, including some awkward ones where he had to remind her that his name was "Lance," not "Luke," that she told him about her dragon. At that moment, Lance knew Alexandra—and all her problems—were suddenly his.

After hearing her tale, he vowed to take care of her, and her dragon as well. Her pretty blue eyes brimmed with tears, and he felt her own heart slip into his hands as she embraced him. For the first time since he arrived at the university, he had felt like a real knight, with a real quest that was worth pursuing.

Just thinking of her made him feel more alive, and even more awake.

"Alexandra is not like any princess, you know, Percy," Lance said, as they headed for Torroa. "She's so kind, and so passionate about making the world a better place. And she's so talented. I read her latest scroll and found it very enlightening. I know she is pretty upset about everything that happened yesterday, but the Holy Grail will cheer her up. You'll see."

Percy was too distracted, nipping at a passing fairy, to respond.

Lance laughed at the fluttering creature, smaller than the size of his hand, as it taunted his silly partner.

"I see you're still talking to animals."

Lance briefly lost the confidence in his steps as he turned to face the witch suddenly beside him. Her dark eyes narrowed, drawing her skin more tightly across her narrow face.

Lance groaned, briefly allowing himself to feel the full weight of his remaining fatigue. The witch, Lady Nesbitt, had been a neighbor of his ever since he had moved to Torroa, and she never had anything nice to say to him, especially since Percy had unintentionally peed all over a patch of her forbidden posies. Since that day, she never missed the opportunity to remind him he was far from perfect—and that he owed her a growing sum, for Percy's other damage.

Too bad there is no fairy to distract the old, bitter witch, Lance thought tiredly. But he smiled, regardless, for a knight-errant was more than just a man who fought for his princess. He was a man of goodwill toward all. "It seems I am, but I can assure you Percy's responses are quite pleasant, especially compared to some," Lance replied. "I wish you a pleasant day as well, Lady Nesbitt."

He waited until he was several yards past her before adding, "In hell," because even a knight-errant could dabble in sarcasm when the occasion called for it.

"As long as you drag that beast around, I'm already living in hell," the witch yelled back.

Lance sighed. It figured that the old witch had enchanted ears.

He glanced back at her, watching as her wild, white hair stuck out in knots from underneath her pointed hat. Her skin was ghostly gray, and her long, flowing robes bounced over her plump, squatted figure to give her the perfect malevolent aura. He cocked an eyebrow at her. "I already gave you my sincerest apologies for your flowers."

Lady Nesbitt said, "You still owe me the money."

"I have not the time, nor the funds, to handle the matter," Lance replied. "I am on a quest today, for my beloved. I will have to get it to you at a different time."

"You're on another quest?" Lady Nesbitt scrunched up her face in disapproval. "That's the third one this month! If that princess of yours needs you to run around for her, I'd hardly call that a good match for you."

"So good of you to be concerned for my heart, Lady Nesbitt."

"I'm more concerned with my money!"

"As with my heart, my money is mine, and neither of them deserve giving you any consideration."

Lady Nesbitt yelled, "Don't make me take it up with the magistrate!"

"I doubt you will bother the magistrate at all, considering the other illegal flora you keep around." But even as he rebuffed her arguments, Lance felt his footsteps hurry even faster down the path. Lady Nesbitt was giving him her evil eye, and he did not want to be caught in any supernatural crosshairs.

"Come, Percy," he said, tugging on Percy's bridle. "Let's journey through the woods. It is a quicker way to the Holy Grail, and Lady Nesbitt will be hidden from our sight."

Percy willingly complied, and Lance wondered if even Percy knew that a priest performing an exorcism would be of more help to Lady Nesbitt's situation than a magistrate calling for his arrest.

The forest eagerly welcomed them, and Lance found relief from not only Lady Nesbitt's stark scorn, but from the sun's glare as well. He pulled off his helmet as he made his way through the woods.

There was no clear trail set before him, but he knew his way well enough—or so he would insist to himself. At times, he saw many crossroads between broken branches and fallen trees; other times, he was sure he had passed that way before. And despite his belief that all he needed to get through the thrush was the thought of his beloved princess, he soon found himself lost and unsure.

"Alexandra is counting on us, Percy," Lance said with a yawn, sitting down long enough to remove the pebbles from his boots and pull the broken twigs out of Percy's mane. "Still … perhaps I should have brought my sword."

A voice called out to him. "Are you lost again, Sir Knight?"

Lance turned around and groaned to himself. *First the witch, and now the ogre,* he thought. "How are you today, Judd?"

In all the time Lance had known Judd, the resident homeless ogre of Torroa, he was always surprised at the sight of his flashy spectacles and his knitted hat. He seemed more like a lecturer who got lost on his way to the university than one who preferred the creature comforts of the woods. "I'm not lost, Judd."

"But I am in a mood for a game," Judd replied, pushing his glasses up on his long, crooked nose. "And I am looking for someone to play with me."

"I don't have time to play games today," Lance said. "I'm off on a quest for the Holy Grail, so I can save my princess."

"I heard from some of her friends she needs some saving today," Judd replied. "She has been up in her tower all night. Some have said she was crying, while others insist she has been working, all throughout the night."

Lance nodded somberly. "She had a big project she was working on, and her dragon is back, terrorizing her once more."

Judd rolled his unsympathetic eyes. "She's not the only one who has a dragon, you know."

"It's not like she wanted it," Lance replied, suddenly more tired than ever. It was always hard to explain to someone who did not have to deal with a dragon the way Alexandra did what it was like.

"She should get over it and just kill that thing herself, if she knew what was good for her. But then," Judd replied, "it must be nice to have it around, knowing that if it poops on her floor and claws at her furniture, she has you to come and save the day."

"It is not a problem that can just be solved so easily," Lance said quietly. "And you would do well to stop saying such things. You disrespect her, and everyone else who has a dragon problem, when you say things like that."

"But I do respect her. She is a good leader. I just wonder if she respects herself somedays, especially when I hear about how she handles her dragon. It doesn't seem like she is trying that hard to deal with it. Sometimes, I think she even uses it as an excuse." Judd shrugged. "But no matter. I will give you the direction of the Holy Grail, if that is what you seek."

He knew he was lost, but Lance was still skeptical of allowing Judd to help him. "What is the price?"

"When we get there, I'd like a drink."

"I could use one myself," Lance agreed with a yawn. As he considered the ogre's offer, he slowly nodded. "Alright. I agree to your terms."

"Excellent." Judd rubbed his hands together. "Come then, Sir Knight. I will show you the way out of my forest."

Together with Judd, Percy and Lance crossed a small bridge, hopped over small streams, and looped their way through the final tangles of the woods. And there, finally, before him, was the Holy Grail.

It was inside a small, hut-shaped cave, full of wonders and terrors, fraught with possibilities, that Lance finally saw the magical cup.

As he approached, he knew this was everything that he had come for, and it was everything that Alexandra would need. He hurried to tie Percy outside, quickly ushering Judd into the sacred shadows behind him.

His vision blurred as he stepped up to the center pedestal, where the Holy Grail's goodness shined, a beacon of hope to all who were weary, to all who were drained, to all who needed inspiration. Everything else faded away as the sacred chalice, free but costly, called to him.

The cup itself was nondescript; there was no mark or design that signaled its importance. As he approached it, he felt himself pause; the aroma of the cave wrapped around him, welcoming him once more. There was warmth, but far from the overpowering heat of summer. Other sounds could be heard around him as he stood there, but the moment had passed for him to consider them as important as his prize.

"The Holy Grail," he whispered, awed once more that he had made it to this place at last, and he was here, all in order to save his beloved.

Lance glanced down into the cup, dazzled by the swirling patterns of pleasure and the ripples of wonder that jostled against the rim.

The liquid portal before him beckoned to him, and Lance found himself unable to resist the delicious sanctuary the elixir offered.

He put the cup to his lips and drank, and the world around him instantly melted away.

"Come on, Lance, you can't hog all the samples."

Judd's voice cut through his reverie, sharp and fast. Lance sighed into his cup, allowing the bittersweet remnant of his morning coffee to wash away the last of his lingering dreams.

He blinked as he looked around the Holy Grail. The blur of the coffeehouse he'd experienced before was gone. The cave-like shadows of the shaded coffee shop curled around small tables and ducked around corners. All around him, other college students seemed to crowd into his vision, almost to insist upon his attention now that he was awakened enough to give it to them.

Lance looked over toward the counter where a barista was checking her phone messages while she waited for her next customer. Outside, Lance could see Percy, his loyal Labrador, as he waited patiently, tied by the leash to one of the many faded magazine stands scattered throughout Torroa's college town. As a new pair of butterflies passed by, Percy barked cheerfully and wagged his tail.

And then Lance looked back at Judd, who was frowning and tapping his toe impatiently against the coffeehouse floor.

"Well?" Judd demanded. "Are you going to order our coffee or did you get your fill on the last of the coffee samples?"

"Lighten up, Judd," Lance said. With a half-smile, he added, "Don't be such an ogre."

"You said you would get me a drink," Judd replied, pressing his glasses up his nose in irritation.

"No, you said you *wanted* a drink," Lance reminded him. "I didn't say I would pay for it."

"Hey! That's not nice." Judd's eyes darkened. "Especially after you drank all the freebies."

"It's not nice to try to get me to buy you a cup of coffee by withholding directions to the Holy Grail, either," Lance reminded him.

"Come on. You know that the Holy Grail is my favorite coffee house in town." Judd scowled. "Besides, ever since we had that storm two months back, you've been getting lost in the woods on a regular basis. And it's not like I am charging you for my services."

"Just because you live under a bridge in the woods doesn't mean you own them."

"If I'm going to be a serious botanist, living in the woods is ideal while I'm working on my undergrad," Judd replied. "Besides, do you know how many hits I get on my blog each month? Millions. And the grocery store here in Torroa lets me have free avocados."

"And yet you still want me to pay for your coffee?"

"Free avocados only go so far." Judd crossed his arms over his chest. "Come on, you can afford it. I heard you got another scholarship for next semester."

"The Knights know they need me on the team," Lance said, tossing the empty sample cup into a wastebasket on the other side of the café. "But on the downside, my position on the basketball team doesn't get free avocados."

"Show off. I should've known better than to try to help one of Torroa's Knights. All of you jocks are just a bunch of smug jerks."

"Calm down, Judd," Lance said, finally unable to stop his laughter. "Fortunately for you, and maybe unfortunately for me, we're friends, and I was teasing you. So I'll buy you a cup today. But I can't stay and play checkers with you. Alexandra needs some coffee, too."

"It's *chess*, Lance. *Chess*, not checkers."

"Well, right now, it is *check, please*, because I have to get going."

"That was lame."

"Well, we're even then," Lance said. "But ultimately, I am still the winner. I'm going to see Alex, after all."

"Your princess awaits," Judd said, reluctantly agreeing. He gave an indignant huff. "I don't know how the smartest girl in our graduating class ended up deciding she liked you."

"It was a miracle, that's for sure," Lance said with a grin as Judd rolled his eyes.

Even if Judd thought he was playing, Lance knew he meant every word.

It was a miracle that Alexandra had granted him that first date, after all the trouble he had gone through to sit next to her in their few shared classes, and after all the attempts to get her to hang out with his friends at the basketball games and the Holy Grail.

He had come to Torroa College for an education and some direction, but he had ended up falling in love and finding that love provided its own sense of purpose and destination. Alex was his college sweetheart, and he loved her.

I love her. I love her, and I want to be there for her.

"Well, she's a bright one," Judd finally said, as he sipped the coffee from his own cup. "But there's no denying she's got some problems."

"It's nothing I can't handle," Lance replied.

But as he left the Holy Grail coffeehouse with two large cups in his hands, he could not stop a shiver from running down his back. Judd had a point—Alex did have her share of problems.

Alex was waiting for him, and that likely meant her dragon was, too.

As soon as Lance opened the door to Alexandra's apartment, he felt a creeping sense of weariness come over him despite his earlier cup of coffee at the café. *Judd was right about the bad news*, he thought. *I'll bet anything she's more upset than he realized, though.*

Of course, he thought, he hadn't realized how bad it was, either.

"Alex?" Lance called, as he stepped into the dark space. His shoe brushed up against a fallen book as he turned on the light.

He whistled, astounded at the sight before him. Books were half-opened, lying on the floor and the couch, and clothes were piled up in different corners. Several half-eaten bowls of cereal were placed around the room, almost like decorative pieces.

Lance stepped forward carefully, while Percy trotted around the room, sniffing eagerly.

"Wow. This is a mess."

"Lance? S'at you?"

He turned toward the desk shoved beside the bookcase, where Alexandra was slowly waking up. He saw at once Alex's beautiful eyes were violet, the lack of sleep running red into the blue of her irises, all held in suspension with an abundance of sadness. The minx-colored tresses of her hair were locked up in knots, and her face was crossed with several red dashes from falling asleep on her keyboard.

"Princess," Lance murmured. Putting the coffee aside, he walked over to her and knelt down beside her. "What happened?"

"They … rejected … my manuscript," she said, each word punctuated by a pause. "A hundred thousand words, and none of them are good enough to be published." Her arms folded around her face as she turned away from him.

Lance reached out and took her into his arms, holding onto her while she struggled. Across the room, he could feel the weight of the dragon that stalked her waiting for a moment to strike.

He had to protect her—but this was a pain he could not stop. He knew that. It was a pain born of love, a hope that was lost, and he could do nothing to right her heart's brokenness.

If he could not stop her heart from breaking, it was up to him to begin to pick up the pieces.

"I know it is your dream to be published," Lance murmured into her hair as he held her. "I know you want to change the world with your words."

"It's all I've ever wanted," she sobbed. "I'm at the top of my class. I'll be graduating college a year early. I've spent years working on this story. Why isn't it good enough?"

Lance just held her for several long moments, letting her alternate between anger at the world, frustration at the publishing house, and sadness at her rejection.

"I'm just not good, I guess," Alexandra whimpered. "I guess I'm not really that good of a writer at all. I'm a failure."

"Hey," Lance objected. "You are not a failure. This is only the beginning, Alex. This is the first time you've submitted a book. You've had articles published online and short stories in magazines. You're a good writer. *I* even read your stuff, and I liked it, even though it's clearly too girly for me to read on a regular basis."

He heard her swallow a laugh and gave her a small smile. "You just have to give yourself time."

Lance leaned in and gave her forehead a kiss, and at that moment, he felt the dragon seem to step back, ever so slightly.

"What if I never make it as a writer?" Alex whispered. "What if this is all I have to look forward to for the rest of my life?"

"I will still love you," Lance told her. "And I will still be here to hold you and tell you that I love you. And … " He reached over, using his long arms to take hold of the coffee cup he had purchased earlier. "Here. I will bring you your own Holy Grail coffee cup to cry in, while I help you clean up your apartment."

Alex finally gave him a smile in return. "I guess it's gotten pretty bad around here, huh?"

"Percy doesn't mind," Lance assured her, as he started collecting the laundry and carrying the plates to the sink. He tried to think of a way to ask her if she had taken her medication today. When he could not find a way to bring it up in a way he was sure would not hurt her, he went back to focusing on cleaning.

Lance worked continuously, stopping every once in a while to nudge Alex to drink her coffee, as he told her about his morning run-in with Mrs. Nesbitt next door, and Judd's apparent obsession with chess, and everything else he could think of that would entertain her.

"And I think Percy needs to go to a vet dentist," Lance said. "His breath is nasty, terribly, terribly nasty. I mean, really, is it his dog food that's making his mouth rancid? He woke me up this morning and—"

He looked over at her, expecting her to giggle, only to find her looking at him intently.

"What is it?" he asked.

"Thank you, Lance," she said quietly. "For taking care of me."

He shook his head, brushing her thanks aside. "You're welcome. I'm glad I can help."

Alexandra held the coffee up to her lips, breathing in the reassuring aroma of the bitter beans. "Thank you for taking care of the dragon, too," she whispered.

Lance took her hand and squeezed it reassuringly. "I promised you when we started dating I would take care of you," he said. "I know your depression has never been easy to deal with, and there is no quick fix. But I am sure you will be published one day, and I'm not going to let your dragon stop you. Even if you are the one who has to fight it, I will be here to keep the rest of your world intact."

Alexandra sighed, this time with a hint of happiness. "You really are my knight in shining armor, aren't you?"

"You have my oath on it, beloved Princess." And then he held her there for a long time, before he leaned down and kissed her, tasting her tears as they mixed with the remnant of her coffee.

A Knight's Quest for the Holy Grail

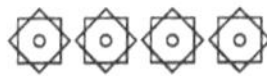

GRAPHIC NOVEL EDITION

STORY BY

C. S. Johnson

ILLUSTRATIONS BY

Fammy Purnama

BLAH !!
WHAT HAVE YOU BEEN EATING, PERCY?
ALRIGHT, I'M GETTING UP.
BACK FROM ME, YOU FEARSOME BRUTE.
ALRIGHT, ALRIGHT,
I KNOW YOU'RE HUNGRY.
I SUPPOSE YOU'RE RIGHT,
ANYWAY, PERCY ...
WE PROMISED THE PRINCESS WE WOULD SAVE HER TODAY.

AND EVERY KNIGHT KNOWS
THERE IS NOTHING
MORE IMPORTANT THAN
COMPLETING HIS QUEST.
SET
PRINCESS
ALEXANDRA
...

I AM COMING FOR YOU
I MISS YOU SO MUCH PRINCESS
LET'S GO, PERCY!

UNIVERSITY OF TORROA
3 years ago
I COULD NOT NAME THE EXACT MOMENT I HAD FALLEN IN LOVE WITH HER
BUT I KNEW THE MOMENT WHEN I COULD NO LONGER SEPARATE MY HAPPINESS FROM HERS.

IT WAS SEVERAL DAYS AND MANY DISCUSSIONS LATER, ...
I'M SORRY !!
OOPS ..
ARE YOU OKAY, LUKE?
... INCLUDING SOME AWKWARD ONES WHERE I HAD TO REMIND HER THAT MY NAME WAS "LANCE" NOT "LUKE,"
SHE ALSO TOLD ME ABOUT HER DRAGON.
I KNEW ALEXANDRA
AND ALL HER PROBLEMS ...
... WERE SUDDENLY MINE

NOWADAYS
ALEXANDRA IS NOT LIKE ANY PRINCESS, YOU KNOW, PERCY,
HA.. HA.. HA..
ARE YOU OKAY, PERCY? ... DOES THE FAIRY BOTHER YOU?
SHE'S SO KIND, AND SO PASSIONATE ABOUT MAKING THE WORLD A BETTER PLACE
!?
HA.. HA.. HA.. HA..
I SEE YOU'RE STILL TALKING TO ANIMALS.

LANCE
LADY NESBITT
I WISH YOU A PLEASANT DAY AS WELL, LADY NESBITT
IT SEEMS I AM, BUT I CAN ASSURE YOU PERCY'S RESPONSES ARE QUITE PLEASANT, ESPECIALLY COMPARED TO SOME
AS LONG AS YOU DRAG THAT BEAST AROUND, I'M ALREADY LIVING IN HELL
IN HELL~

I ALREADY GAVE YOU MY SINCEREST APOLOGIES FOR YOUR FLOWERS.
YOU STILL OWE ME THE MONEY
I HAVE NOT THE TIME, NOR THE FUNDS, TO HANDLE THE MATTER
I AM ON A QUEST TODAY, FOR MY BELOVED. I WILL HAVE TO GET IT TO YOU AT A DIFFERENT TIME.
YOU'RE ON ANOTHER QUEST?
THAT'S THE THIRD ONE THIS MONTH! IF THAT PRINCESS OF YOURS NEEDS YOU TO RUN AROUND FOR HER, I'D HARDLY CALL THAT A GOOD MATCH FOR YOU.
SO GOOD OF YOU TO BE CONCERNED FOR MY HEART LADY NESBIT
I'M MORE CONCERNED WITH MY MONEY!
AS WITH MY HEART, MY MONEY IS MINE, AND NEITHER OF THEM DESERVE GIVING YOU ANY CONSIDERATION

DON'T MAKE ME TAKE IT UP WITH THE MAGISTRATE!
I DOUBT YOU WILL BOTHER THE MAGISTRATE AT ALL, CONSIDERING THE OTHER ILLEGAL FLORA YOU KEEP AROUND.
COME PERCY!
JOURNEY THROUGH THE WOODS. IT IS A QUICKER WAY TO THE HOLY GRAIL

ALEXANDRA IS COUNTING ON US, PERCY
HOAM~
STILL ... PERHAPS I SHOULD HAVE BROUGHT MY SWORD.
SET
ARE YOU LOST AGAIN, SIR KNIGHT?

HOW ARE YOU TODAY, JUDD?
KHU KHU KHU
B E T
TEP!
I'M NOT LOST, JUDD.
BUT I AM IN A MOOD FOR A GAME,
AND I AM LOOKING FOR SOMEONE TO PLAY WITH ME.
I DON'T HAVE TIME TO PLAY GAMES TODAY
I'M OFF ON A QUEST FOR THE HOLY GRAIL, SO I CAN SAVE MY PRINCESS.
HEARD FROM SOME OF HER FRIENDS SHE NEEDS SOME SAVING TODAY
SHE HAS BEEN UP IN HER TOWER
ALL NIGHT. SOME HAVE SAID SHE WAS CRYING, WHILE OTHERS INSIST SHE HAS BEEN WORKING, ALL THROUGHOUT THE NIGHT.

SHE HAD A BIG PROJECT SHE WAS WORKING ON, AND HER DRAGON IS BACK,
TERRORIZING HER ONCE MORE.
SHE'S NOT THE ONLY ONE WHO HAS A DRAGON, YOU KNOW.
IT'S NOT LIKE SHE WANTED IT
SHE SHOULD GET OVER IT AND JUST KILL THAT THING HERSELF, IF SHE KNEW WHAT WAS GOOD FOR HER.
BUT THEN,
...IT MUST BE NICE TO HAVE IT AROUND, KNOWING THAT IF IT POOPS ON HER FLOOR AND CLAWS AT HER FURNITURE, SHE HAS YOU TO COME AND SAVE THE DAY.
IT IS NOT A PROBLEM THAT CAN JUST BE SOLVED SO EASILY

AND YOU WOULD DO WELL TO STOP SAYING SUCH THINGS. YOU DISRESPECT HER, AND EVERYONE ELSE WHO HAS A DRAGON PROBLEM, WHEN YOU SAY THINGS LIKE THAT.
BUT I DO RESPECT HER. SHE IS A GOOD LEADER.
I JUST WONDER IF SHE RESPECTS HERSELF SOMEDAYS,
ESPECIALLY WHEN I HEAR ABOUT HOW SHE HANDLES HER DRAGON.
BUT NO MATTER. I WILL GIVE YOU THE DIRECTION OF THE HOLY GRAIL, IF THAT IS WHAT YOU SEEK.
WHAT IS THE PRICE?
WHEN WE GET THERE, I'D LIKE A DRINK.

I COULD USE ONE MYSELF,
ALRIGHT. I AGREE TO YOUR TERMS.
EXCELLENT.
COME THEN, SIR KNIGHT.
I WILL SHOW YOU THE WAY OUT OF MY FOREST.

TEP!
WE HAVE REACHED THE DESTINATION, SIR KNIGHT

THE HOLY GRAIL ..

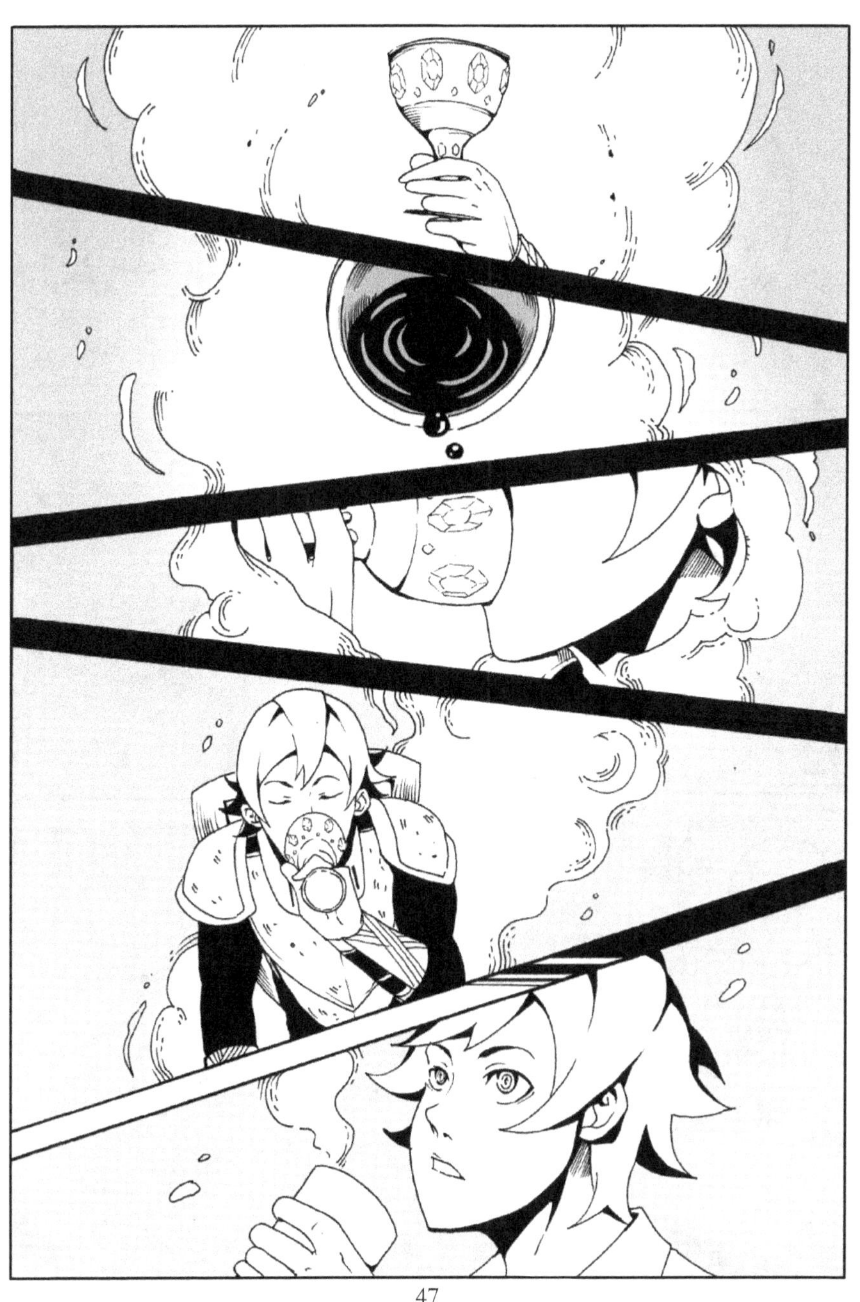

COME ON, LANCE, YOU CAN'T HOG ALL THE SAMPLES.
WELL?
THE HOLY GRAIL
He Brews Holy Beans
Knights
ARE YOU GOING TO ORDER OUR COFFEE OR DID YOU GET YOUR FILL ON THE LAST OF THE COFFEE SAMPLES?

LIGHTEN UP, JUDD, DON'T BE SUCH AN OGRE.
YOU SAID YOU WOULD GET ME A DRINK
NO, YOU SAID YOU WANTED A DRINK
I DIDN'T SAY I WOULD PAY FOR IT.
HEY! THAT'S NOT NICE.
ESPECIALLY AFTER YOU DRANK ALL THE FREEBIES.
IT'S NOT NICE TO TRY TO GET ME TO BUY YOU A CUP OF COFFEE BY WITHHOLDING DIRECTIONS TO THE HOLY GRAIL, EITHER
Knights
Knights

COME ON. YOU KNOW THAT THE HOLY GRAIL IS MY FAVORITE COFFEE HOUSE IN TOWN.
BESIDES, EVER SINCE WE HAD THAT STORM TWO MONTHS BACK, YOU'VE BEEN GETTING LOST IN THE WOODS ON A REGULAR BASIS.
AND IT'S NOT LIKE I AM CHARGING YOU FOR MY SERVICES.
HOLY
He Brews
Holy Beans
JUST BECAUSE YOU LIVE UNDER A BRIDGE IN THE WOODS DOESN'T MEAN YOU OWN THEM.
AND YET YOU STILL WANT ME TO PAY FOR YOUR COFFEE?
IF I'M GOING TO BE A SERIOUS BOTANIST, LIVING IN THE WOODS IS IDEAL WHILE I'M WORKING ON MY UNDERGRAD
BESIDES, DO YOU KNOW HOW MANY HITS I GET ON MY BLOG EACH MONTH? MILLIONS. AND THE GROCERY STORE HERE IN TORROA LETS ME HAVE FREE AVOCADOS.

WELL, RIGHT NOW, IT IS "CHECK, PLEASE", BECAUSE I HAVE TO GET GOING.
THAT WAS LAME.
WELL, WE'RE EVEN THEN,
BUT ULTIMATELY, I AM STILL THE WINNER.
I'M GOING TO SEE ALEX, AFTER ALL.
Knights
YOUR PRINCESS AWAITS
TEP!

ALEX?
!
Knights
Knights
TEP!
WOW. THIS IS A MESS.
CLACK!
Knights

LANCE?
S'AT YOU?
PRINCESS
WHAT
HAPPENED?
THEY
...
REJECTED
...
MY
MANUSCRIPT
A HUNDRED
THOUSAND
WORDS
AND NONE
OF THEM
ARE GOOD
ENOUGH
TO BE
PUBLISHED.

I KNOW IT IS YOUR DREAM TO BE PUBLISHED
I KNOW YOU WANT TO CHANGE THE WORLD WITH YOUR WORDS.
Knights
IT'S ALL I'VE EVER WANTED
I'M AT THE TOP OF MY CLASS. I'LL BE GRADUATING COLLEGE A YEAR EARLY.
I'VE SPENT YEARS WORKING ON THIS STORY.
WHY ISN'T IT GOOD ENOUGH?

I'M JUST NOT GOOD, I GUESS .... I GUESS I'M NOT REALLY THAT GOOD OF A WRITER AT ALL. I'M A FAILURE.
HEY,
YOU ARE NOT A FAILURE. THIS IS ONLY THE BEGINNING, ALEX
HIKS
HIKS
THIS IS THE FIRST TIME YOU'VE SUBMITTED A BOOK. YOU'VE HAD ARTICLES PUBLISHED ONLINE AND SHORT STORIES IN MAGAZINES. YOU'RE A GOOD WRITER.
I EVEN READ YOUR STUFF, AND I LIKED IT, EVEN THOUGH IT'S CLEARLY TOO GIRLY FOR ME TO READ ON A REGULAR BASIS.
YOU JUST HAVE TO GIVE YOURSELF TIME.
Knights

WHAT IF I NEVER MAKE IT AS A WRITER?
WHAT IF THIS IS ALL I HAVE TO LOOK FORWARD TO FOR THE REST OF MY LIFE?
I WILL STILL LOVE YOU
AND I WILL STILL BE HERE TO HOLD YOU AND TELL YOU THAT I LOVE YOU.
AND ....
HERE. I WILL BRING YOU YOUR OWN HOLY GRAIL COFFEE CUP TO CRY IN,
WHILE I HELP YOU CLEAN UP YOUR APARTMENT.

I GUESS IT'S GOTTEN PRETTY BAD AROUND HERE, HUH?
PERCY DOESN'T MIND
AND I THINK PERCY NEEDS TO GO TO A VET DENTIST
HIS BREATH IS NASTY, TERRIBLY, TERRIBLY NASTY. I MEAN, REALLY, IS IT HIS DOG FOOD THAT'S MAKING HIS MOUTH RANCID?
HE WOKE ME UP THIS MORNING AND ....
WHAT IS IT?
Knights

YOU REALLY ARE MY KNIGHT IN SHINING ARMOR,
AREN'T YOU?
YOU HAVE MY OATH ON IT, BELOVED PRINCESS.
Knights

C. S. Johnson is the author of several young adult sci-fi and fantasy novels, including *The Starlight Chronicles* series, the *Once Upon a Princess* saga, and the *Divine Space Pirates* trilogy. With a gift for sarcasm and an apologetic heart, she currently lives in Atlanta with her family.

Please read on for a sample of *The Heights of Perdition*, the first book in The Divine Space Pirates Trilogy, a science fiction romance series from C. S. Johnson.

In an apocalyptic future, Aerie St. Cloud and Exton Shepherd were on opposing sides. But after their accidental encounter, their lives—and the lives of their friends, family, and nations—will never be the same.

THANK YOU FOR PICKING UP THIS BOOK!

To Get *Awakening* (A Special Christmas Episode of The *Starlight Chronicles*) for Free,
Click Here

Download It At:
https://www.csjohnson.me/awakening

SAMPLE CHAPTER

Chapter 1 from

THE HEIGHTS

OF

PERDITION

BOOK ONE OF *THE DIVINE SPACE PIRATES*

♦♦♦♦

C. S. Johnson

♦1♦

At just the right angle, the dark blue and white orb, suspended in a sea of invisible shadows, held in place by a faith as impossible to believe in as it was to see, fit nicely between his fingers. Outside his window, Earth looked small and fragile, seemingly innocent, and mostly harmless. A hollowness slipped between his thumb and forefinger as he squashed them together, crushing the blueberry-sized circle.

Amused by the irony of the forced perspective before him, a rare, genuine smile formed on Exton Shepherd's face.

It was, he decided, almost a shame no one else was around to witness such an unusual event. He smooshed his fingers together, imagining the world completely decimated into dust.

But then, he recalled, he'd given plenty of smiles earlier, as all the hubbub went on about the ship. Surely the crew, his hodgepodge of adopted family and coworkers, would have been satisfied with those, even though they were inauthentic at best and mocking at worst.

Duty sometimes demanded playing happy. Exton knew that, and he followed it, even in instances he loathed.

Like today.

Between the thirteenth and fifteenth sunrises of his day, he'd watched the only other person he truly cared for in all the world—no, he mentally corrected himself, in all the universe—pledge her love, heart, and life to another man.

It was heartbreaking on some levels, but strangely freeing, too.

The wedding had been quaint, warm, and sweet. Its simplicity suggested nothing of its socially taxing nature.

Exton had no regrets about ducking out as soon as the bride and groom finished their vows and the Ecclesia had pronounced them husband and wife.

Once he had successfully slipped out of sight, Exton proceeded to the Captain's Lounge, the small room he'd claimed as his the day after launching the *Perdition* into space. There was little to be said of the room's comfort; it was more like a tall elevator shaft than a room, empty of everything but the coldness of space and a small window hidden up near the far end. More than once, Exton wondered if he'd found a kind of kinship with it; hollow and bleak, with a tiny view looking out toward the fleeing horizon.

It was there, on a window seat built into the windowpane, where Exton tucked his legs under his chin and entered into his own world of privacy, where he was free to be who he wanted, even if it was for only a moment.

As captain of the ship, he didn't want his crew to see him in one of his more melancholy moods.

His frown returned when he opened his fingers again, only to see Earth was still hanging in space before him, its silence mocking and spiteful. Rearranging his hand, he made it seem like he was carrying the earth in the palm. Fleetingly, he toyed with the idea of pretending to toss the small pearl away into the dark recesses of space, into an imaginary hell.

But he knew that would not work.

Exton knew two things with startling clarity and unshakable certainty: The first was that hell was real, and the second was that it was his home.

"Having fun?" a voice asked from below him.

"Huh?" Exton jerked around in surprise, nearly falling off the window ledge. "Come on, Emery, don't do that," he groaned, while the young woman dressed all in white only laughed. His balance, already compromised by the pull of the starship's gravity, faltered again as Exton tried to adjust himself. "You know I don't like it when people interrupt me, especially when I'm here."

"But it's my wedding day," Emery insisted. "And I'd like to have a dance with the ship's captain before the night shift starts. Come on, we're up first."

Exton gave up on staying by the window and jumped down as gracefully as he could. "All the shifts up here are technically the night shift," he grumbled.

"Some would say we live in perpetual day up here on the *Perdition*," Emery offered, her voice gentle even as she maintained her stance. "Sunrise and sunset are only ninety-two minutes apart for us now, when we're this close to Earth."

"Sunrises and sunsets do not make day and night up here," Exton told her, touching his forehead.

Emery reached out and took his hand, before she placed it over his heart. "I think your problem is too much night in here, not out there." She turned her attention back to the window, where six inches of steel-grade glass separated them from the vacuum of space.

Exton followed her gaze, wondering if she was looking for any sign of familiarity from their old home. He watched as the end of the ocean braced itself against the shore of the Old Republic; he felt his memory pull him in, and he could see it clearly inside his mind.

The chill of the old mountains where he would go work and play with his father, the spray of the salt water on his transport module, the warmth of his mother's arms as she welcomed him home from school—all of it embraced him, surrounding him and penetrating into the deep recesses of his heart.

And then there was pain, and then it was gone.

Exton shook his head. "I know it seems like a long time has passed, but it's time to cause the URS some trouble. It's almost the anniversary, you know."

"I know," she replied. A sudden sadness appeared in her gaze, and Exton wondered if she had been reminiscing as well.

Pushing aside his grief, he straightened his shoulders. "I have a plan that will really make them sorry this year, Em."

"I know you're a man of your word," Emery replied, "but I'm not sure it will be enough to convince them to give us what we want."

"They already cannot give us what we want." Exton shrugged. "Our game was never for power. It was for meaning."

"It's not a game, Exton."

"I know it's not!" Out of the corner of his eye, he saw Emery flinch. "I know it's not," he repeated carefully, reverting to his usual, detached tone. "It's not our fault that it became a quest for survival, Emery. I know that even more than you do."

"If it's survival you want," Emery scoffed, "there's no point in selling your soul in the process."

Before Exton could assure Emery he had no soul left that was worth saving, let alone selling, he stopped. Happy times, he reminded himself.

Emery's wedding was a special occasion, one that had excited her for the past several months, offering a glimmer of hope on a horizon of gloom and turmoil. Exton was determined not to let the past rob him—or her—of anything else, so long as it was in his power. "You're right," he acquiesced, momentarily giving in.

Emery smiled brightly, and Exton suddenly had a hard time believing she was only two years younger than he was. At twenty-two, she seemed much more innocent than the figure that gazed back at him when he looked in the mirror.

He slipped his hand out from under hers, before taking and squeezing it. "Are you sure you wouldn't like to have the first dance with your new husband?"

"Tyler is my heart's desire," Emery told him firmly, "but you will always be my hero."

Exton grimaced. He knew he was no hero. "It would be a shame to waste your time with me."

"Time with you is not a waste."

"Did Tyler approve of changing up the dancing order? The man might be in love, but there's no need to make him prove to be the fool."

"Hey, Tyler's your commander, and your best friend," Emery objected. "You know he's not a fool."

"Not where it concerns you. He would be smart to correct that, and I have been telling him since he received approval from the Ecclesia to start courting you," Exton told her. He gave her a devious look. "Should I make him walk the plank?"

Emery frowned and searched the darkened shadows of his face. "That's not funny, Exton."

"I know."

They walked in silence for a few moments before Exton spoke once more. "I don't want to dance. No offense, Em."

"Traditionally, it was the daughter's duty to dance with her father, first." Emery smiled. "But that's more of a cultural thing I've read about from the Old Republic."

"Yes, I remember that," Exton agreed. "Ironic, how the Revolutionary States would be appalled by it now."

Of course, he recalled, even the idea of using the term "father" might have some of the more militant protestors up in arms, as the beloved Daddy Dictator of the URS, Grant Osgood, did not encourage familial relationships, unless such feelings were directed toward government.

"If the URS is against it, you should be more inclined to appease me, then," Emery contended.

There was a breath of silence and stillness before Exton responded. "I'm not our father," he scoffed.

"You're more like him than you might wish."

As Exton scowled at her, Emery pointed her finger at him accusingly. "See? You even have the same exasperated look he used to get when he was frustrated."

"I'll have to take your word for it." Exton shrugged, scratching his head. He frowned as he realized it had been some time since he'd gotten a haircut. His father used to do the same thing, especially when he was planning his next engineering endeavor. Exton suddenly wondered if it was his own scruffy locks that had been making him shrink back from mirrors of late.

He missed his father too much to want to see him staring out of the mirror from the other side of the grave.

Emery chuckled again, drawing him out of his thoughts. "Well, I know at least one trait you share with him. He had a hard time telling me no to anything I wanted, if memory serves."

"You look too much like Mom for me to say no," Exton admitted. "I'm sure he had the same problem, but that's one I'm more willing to share with him."

With her dark brown hair, blue-green eyes, and petite form, Emery was the living memory of their mother. She even had the same dimple hovering above the left corner of her lips, a trait Exton knew was the extent of their common features. Their father's blue eyes, as clear and sharp as ice, had passed to him, along with his height, broad shoulders, and black hair.

"He always did want me to follow in his footsteps," Exton muttered as they headed out of the Captain's Lounge. "But I'm not sure he would have enjoyed the ghost of Captain Chainsword, the infamous space lumberjack pirate."

"I don't think he would have liked it, given how much he derided you for enjoying those fantasy adventures you used to read."

"It seemed fitting at the time, to create a new role for him to play, along with the rest of us."

"I suppose." Emery shrugged. "But Papa was a brilliant engineer, same as you, and a good man. I'm not sure he would have liked your emphasis on piracy and power."

"For the most part, I think you are right," Exton agreed. "But he was too idealistic by far. That was what got him killed." He looked out a nearby window, where, even as he could no longer see Earth, he still felt the pull of its shadow.

"In hindsight, you would prove to be correct on that point."

"That is why I will not make the same mistake as he did. While *Paradise* is out of reach, *Perdition* will do what it can to ensure a better life for us."

"And others, too," Emery added proudly.

"Maybe." Exton shrugged. "I only have a duty to you, and you're technically Tyler's problem now. Anyone else is just extra."

"Your duty to me hasn't ended."

Exton rolled his eyes. "I'm going to dance with you, aren't I? What else is there?"

"Your duty to me might include a dance tonight, but I wish for you to find someone you would love as I love Tyler." She smiled. "Someone you can spend your life trying to make happy."

"Even as life makes me miserable?"

Emery frowned and sighed. "I don't know why you do that."

"Do what?"

"Make it impossible for yourself to be happy."

"Happiness is fleeting, remember?" Exton rolled his eyes. "Even the leaders of the Ecclesia would agree with me there."

"They don't often agree with you, especially when it comes to your mandates," Emery concurred. "The only reason they would on this account is because the phrasing is vague enough to seem to agree on the meaning." She narrowed her gaze. "And the practice."

Exton wrinkled his nose. "We've been up here for too long if you know me so well."

"I still prefer this to when we were off at different universities, working on our studies," Emery admitted with a thoughtful smile. "But as for the argument, you don't seem to agree with the Ecclesia a whole lot, either. You don't share most of their beliefs. I find it hard to believe that you would try to garner support from among their teachings."

"Their teachings on wisdom and life, and how it should be, I respect. But it's different when you're trying to manage a pirate starship and ruin an empire."

"Not to mention when you insist so stubbornly on remaining miserable."

"I *am* going back to your wedding celebration, aren't I?" Exton groaned. "Please don't push it, Em. You know how I feel. If God would grant your wish for me, if he wanted so much for me to be 'happy,' he could have let me 'fall in love' with someone on the *Perdition*, like you and Tyler. But even when we send our smaller ships down to Earth for supplies, see Aunt Patty, or attack the URS, there's no one there for me. There are only people there who want the protection *Perdition* can offer to political dissents or refugees such as themselves."

After a moment of thought, he added, "Besides, my job is to protect and lead aboard the spaceship. The last thing I need is to be led around by the whims of a woman."

"There's no need to make it sound so deplorable," Emery scoffed, arching an eyebrow at him. "Do you honestly think dealing with the moods of a man are any easier?"

He flashed her a charming grin.

"You don't need to set yourself up for failure like that. We have only been up in space for six years now, hiding in the shadows of all the toxic clouds while playing war games with the URS."

"Not to mention watching destruction of all other sorts go unchecked," Exton added, his voice grim.

"It's not all 'unchecked,'" Emery reminded him. "Exton, you still can't lose hope. God is a supposed to be a god of miracles, remember? We have time."

Exton wondered how his sister could be worried about his heart, when his life, as well all the lives of his crew, faced the bigger risk. It was one thing to be aware of danger, but another to disregard it, especially for something as silly as true love.

He studied Emery's daydreaming smile in silence and decided he had the right of it: As much as she was ever his practical and precise sister, Emery's wedded bliss was affecting her judgment.

Exton was surprised at the sudden stab of jealousy. He squashed it down as he caught sight of the approaching Earth through the galley windows.

Didn't Emery see the coming battle? Exton wondered. *Didn't she feel the haunted air about the starship, with specters of the past lurking around every corner of the* Perdition?

They couldn't outlast the URS forever up in space. While Exton and the Ecclesia had established the *Perdition* as a safe haven over the past few years, it was only a matter of time before the URS would come for them, and he knew it would not be to make peace.

"What is it, Exton?" Emery asked, jolting him out of his gloomy thoughts.

Exton sighed. "It's not like God's just going to dump someone into the ship just for me. You might as well save your breath for dancing, Em."

Thank you for reading! Please leave a review for this book and check out www.csjohnson.me for other books and updates!

www.ingramcontent.com/pod-product-compliance
Lightning Source LLC
Chambersburg PA
CBHW070452170726
48291CB00005B/1722

* 9 7 8 1 9 4 8 4 6 4 3 5 2 *